In Abby's Hands

Wendy A. Lewis   Illustrated by Marilyn Mets & Peter Ledwon

Red Deer Press

It was their own small world
beneath the lace tablecloth,
just big enough for Abby and her dog, Opal.
Abby cupped her hand over Opal's side,
where the warm furry skin stretched tight as
a hug around the pups inside. *To hold a new
life in your hands . . . it fills you with wonder!*
That's what Abby's grandmother, Gran Opal,
used to say.

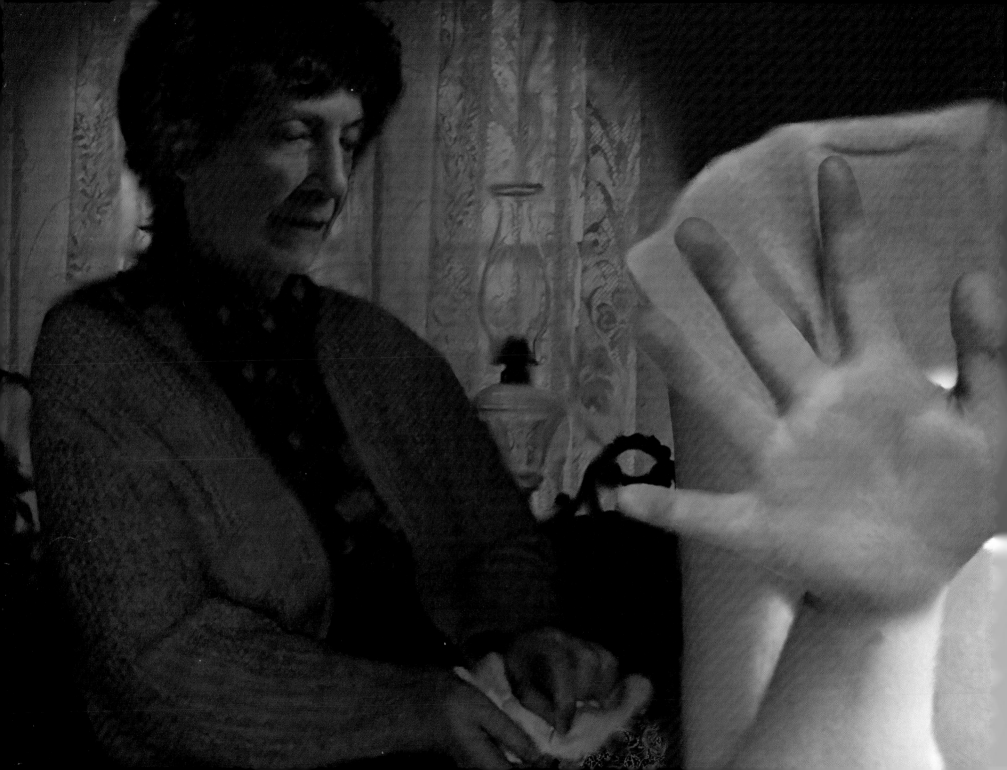

Abby frowned at her stubby fingers and chewed nails. Her hands were nothing like Gran Opal's had been — hands that had made majestic muffins and prize-winning lace tablecloths. Hands that had brought new babies into the world and placed them in their mothers' arms.

Abby's muffins looked like cow plops. She dropped stitches when she tried to crochet. And although she loved watching her mother deliver puppies in their kennel, she rarely helped out. She was afraid of making a mistake.

Grandpa Jack ducked his head under the table.

"Want to help me wrestle the tractor tire into the puppy pen, Ab?"

"Yes!" said Abby. It had been her idea to rescue the tire from the dump. She was sure the puppies would love climbing on it once they were a few weeks old. But Opal set her paw firmly on Abby's knee.

"I don't think Opal wants me to go," Abby laughed.

"Then you should stay." Grandpa Jack ruffled Abby's hair, then patted Opal. "Doesn't it seem like yesterday that she was a pup herself?"

Abby remembered well the wonderful, terrible day that Opal was born. Wonderful because Abby had watched seven plump perfect puppies come into the world. Terrible because miles away, in a strange hospital room, Gran Opal had died.

Abby spent many hours after that cuddling with the puppies, letting their warm bodies cover her like a blanket. Her favorite pup had fur the color of butter and a tail that never stopped wagging. When her mother said they could keep her, Abby knew right away that her name should be Opal.

Opal shifted her weight and sighed. Her eyes pleaded with Abby.

"I wish I *could* help, Opal . . ."

But all Abby could do was gently stroke the bulging puppy shapes in Opal's side. While she stroked, she sang, "He's got the whole world in His hands, He's got the whole world in His hands — "

"WOOF!" Ears cocked, Opal struggled to sit. Outside, the kennel dogs were raising a ruckus.

Then Abby heard her mother scream, "*DAD!*"

Abby raced to the back door. Grandpa Jack was kneeling in the puppy pen, a thin line of blood trickling down his cheek. Abby's mother tried to help him stand, but he sank back to the ground, wincing.

"Dad, what on earth were you thinking," Abby's mother scolded, "lugging that ridiculous tire by yourself?"

The tire!

"Grandpa, I'm sorry!" Abby cried.

"I hope *you* didn't put him up to this, Abby," her mother frowned.

"Not at all," said Grandpa Jack. "It was just me and my two left feet."

"Well *this* left foot needs to go to the hospital," said Abby's mother.

Abby tucked her shoulder under Grandpa Jack's arm and helped him hobble to the truck.

"Grandpa Jack?" she whispered. "Do you . . . need me to be at the hospital? Or . . . "

"No, sweetheart." Grandpa Jack knew that since Gran Opal's illness, Abby was afraid of hospitals.

"Up you go, Dad! You too, Abby," said her mother.

"Abby could stay here, you know," said Grandpa Jack.

"Yes, Mom . . . shouldn't someone be with Opal?"

"The puppies aren't due yet, Abby. But . . . maybe you're right. Opal didn't have much appetite this morning. Keep an eye on her then, and call Jenn if she shows signs of starting labor."

Their neighbor, Jenn, was a dog breeder, too. They could see from her truck in the lane that she was home.

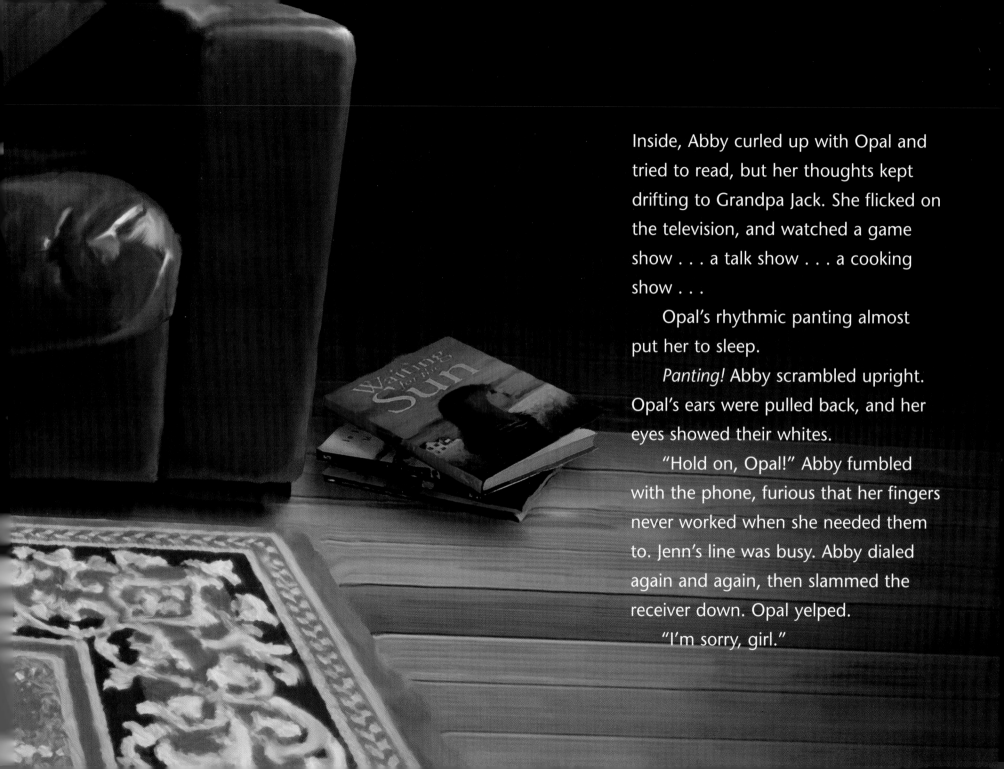

Inside, Abby curled up with Opal and tried to read, but her thoughts kept drifting to Grandpa Jack. She flicked on the television, and watched a game show . . . a talk show . . . a cooking show . . .

Opal's rhythmic panting almost put her to sleep.

Panting! Abby scrambled upright. Opal's ears were pulled back, and her eyes showed their whites.

"Hold on, Opal!" Abby fumbled with the phone, furious that her fingers never worked when she needed them to. Jenn's line was busy. Abby dialed again and again, then slammed the receiver down. Opal yelped.

"I'm sorry, girl."

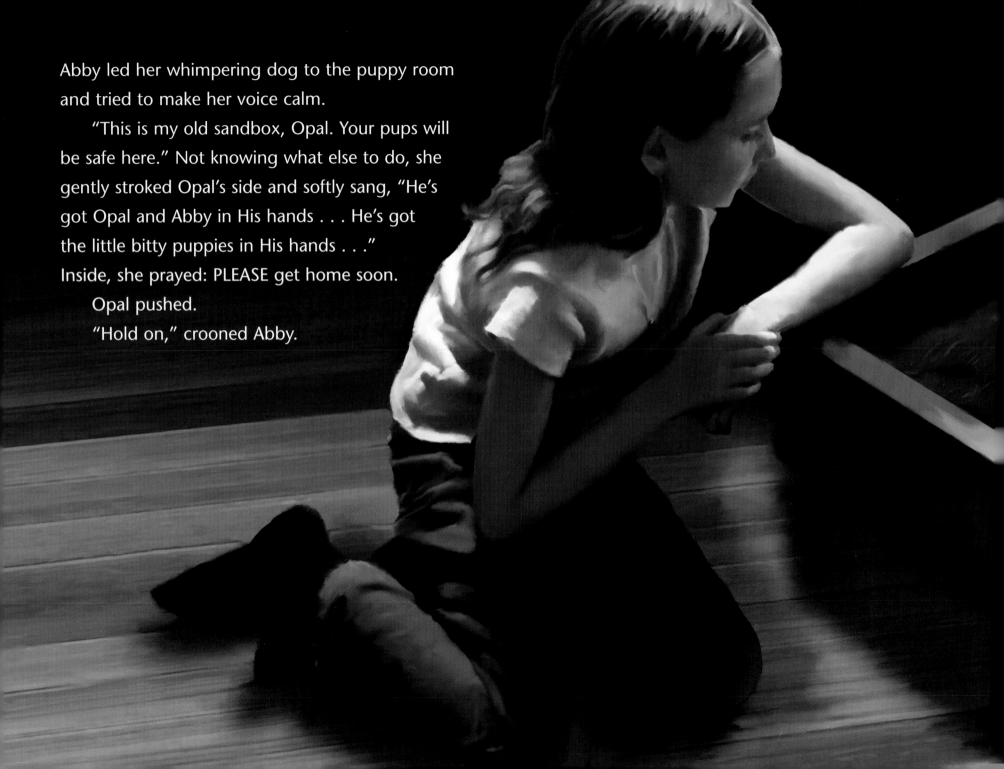

Abby led her whimpering dog to the puppy room
and tried to make her voice calm.

"This is my old sandbox, Opal. Your pups will
be safe here." Not knowing what else to do, she
gently stroked Opal's side and softly sang, "He's
got Opal and Abby in His hands . . . He's got
the little bitty puppies in His hands . . ."
Inside, she prayed: PLEASE get home soon.

Opal pushed.

"Hold on," crooned Abby.

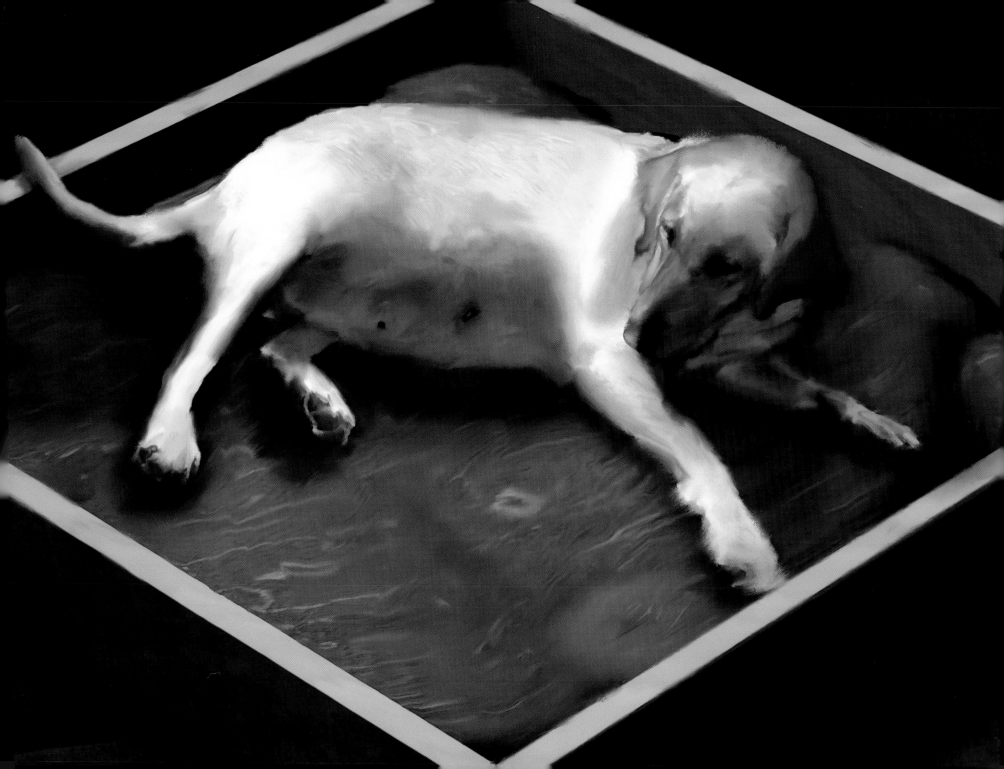

But Opal couldn't hold on.

Out gushed a dark shape inside a cloudy sac. Opal stared at it as if she didn't know what it was. For a moment, Abby froze, too. Then her hands remembered what her head could not, things she had watched her mother do. Quickly, she broke the sac and pulled it away from the puppy's head. His pink mouth gulped silently for air.

"Breathe!" Abby whispered.

She tipped his head down and rubbed his back with a towel. His belly was so slippery against her hand that she was afraid she'd drop him. She adjusted her grip and cleared his mouth with her finger.

"Please . . . *breathe!*"

Finally she felt his chest swell. His tiny heart hammered against her palm. Gran Opal was right. Holding this new life in her hands *did* fill Abby with wonder.

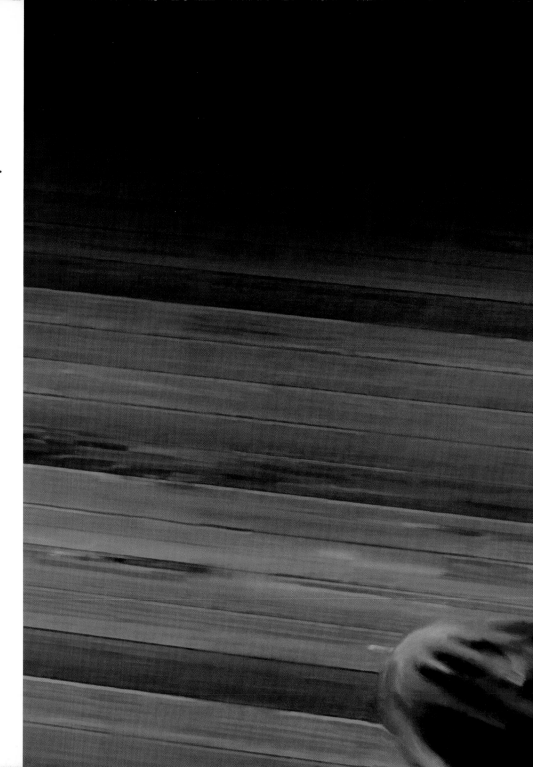

"Opal, look at your beautiful baby!"

Opal sniffed the puppy, then began to lick him clean. The puppy let out a squeaky cry. Abby almost cried, too — with relief.

She watched nervously as Opal bit through the cord that joined the pup to the afterbirth. If the cord bled too much, Abby would have to tie a piece of thread around it, and even her mother had trouble doing that. But the cord looked fine. Abby wiped her hands clean and braced herself for pup number two.

Outside, the truck's horn meep-meeped a jaunty greeting. Through the window, Abby watched her mother help Grandpa Jack down from the truck. His ankle was bandaged, but he grinned when he saw Abby.

"The puppies are coming!" Abby called.

Instantly her mother was there, pushing up her sleeves, checking the new puppy and Opal. Abby waited, twisting the towel in her hands. Had she done the right things? Should she have called Jenn sooner or called her mother at the hospital? Should she have cut the cord herself or tied it with thread?

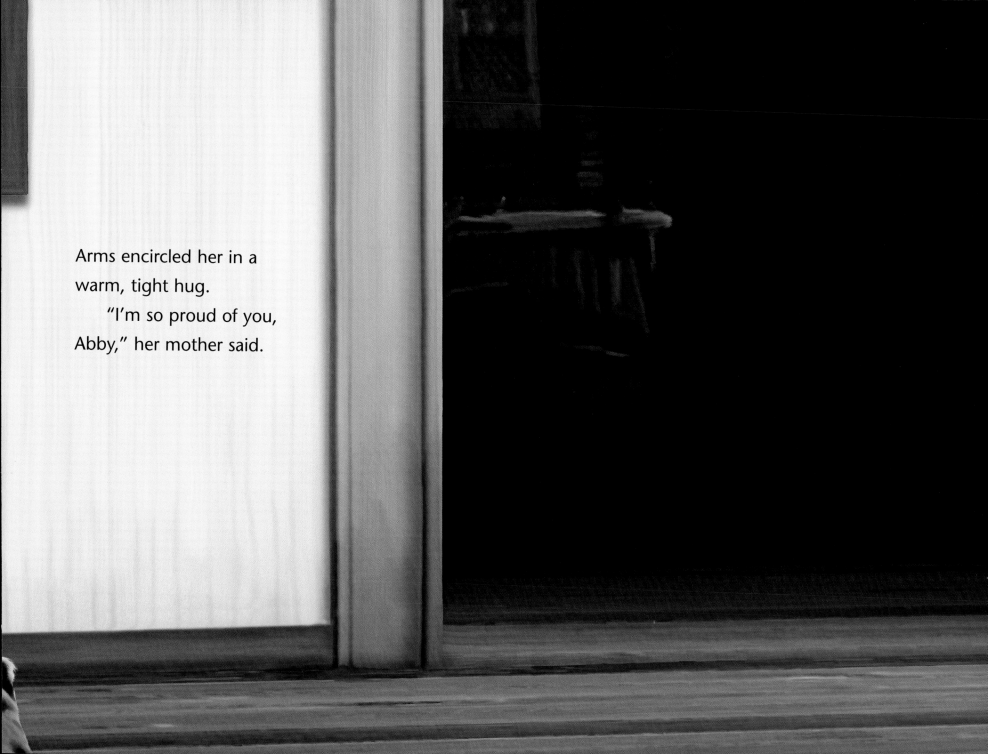

Arms encircled her in a
warm, tight hug.

"I'm so proud of you,
Abby," her mother said.

By evening, Abby had helped her mother deliver seven more puppies. The tiny male that was born first slept soundly, his belly full of warm milk. Carefully Abby lifted him and cradled him like a baby. He snuggled closer but didn't wake up. Even in sleep, he seemed to know that he was safe in Abby's hands.

Northern Lights Books for Children are published by Red Deer Press, 813 MacKimmie Library Tower, 2500 University Drive N.W., Calgary Alberta Canada T2N 1N4
www.reddeerpress.com

Credits
Edited for the Press by Peter Carver
Cover and text design by Blair Kerrigan/Glyphics
Printed and bound in Canada by Friesens for Red Deer Press

Acknowledgments
Financial support provided by the Canada Council, the Department of Canadian Heritage, the Alberta Foundation for the Arts, a beneficiary of the Lottery Fund of the Government of Alberta, and the University of Calgary.

National Library of Canada Cataloguing in Publication Data

Lewis, Wendy, 1966–
In Abby's hands / Wendy Lewis ; illustrator, Marilyn Mets, Peter Ledwon.

(Northern lights books for children)
ISBN 0-88995-282-5

I. Mets, Marilyn. II. Ledwon, Peter. III. Title. IV. Series.
PS8573.E9913I52 2003   jC813'.6   C2003-910215-7
PZ7.L5883In 2003

5 4 3 2 1

For Amelia and Maddy, with heaps of love, for my family as we were then, and for everyone who has ever loved a dog.
– Wendy A. Lewis

For Willa, Larrian and MacKenzie
– Marilyn Mets & Peter Ledwon